Honey, My Rabbit

Written by Barbara Beveridge
Illustrated by Judith DuFour Love

Honey, my rabbit, likes carrots.

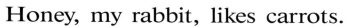

Honey, my rabbit, likes carrots
and cabbage.

Honey, my rabbit, likes carrots
and cabbage and apples.
She likes lettuce, too.

She hops on the grass.
She hops around her house.

She hops around *my* house.

 "A rabbit!" says Kitty.
"I don't like rabbits."

7

But *I* like Honey,
and Honey likes me.